Weekly Reader Books presents

MR. PIG and FAMILY

by Lillian Hoban

An I CAN READ Book

HARPER & ROW, PUBLISHERS

Mr. Pig and Family
Copyright © 1980 by Lillian Hoban
All rights reserved. No part of this book may be
used or reproduced in any manner whatsoever without
written permission except in the case of brief quotations
embodied in critical articles and reviews. Printed in
the United States of America. For information address
Harper & Row, Publishers, Inc., 10 East 53rd Street,
New York, N.Y. 10022. Published simultaneously in
Canada by Fitzhenry & Whiteside Limited, Toronto.
First Edition

Library of Congress Cataloging in Publication Data
Hoban, Lillian.
    Mr. Pig and family.

    (An I can read book)
    SUMMARY: When Mr. Pig marries Selma Pig,
there are many adventures in store for the
new family.
    [1. Pigs—Fiction.   2. Humorous stories]
I. Title.
PZ7.H635Mh 1980   [E]   80-7771
ISBN 0-06-022383-9
ISBN 0-06-022384-7 (lib. bdg.)

LE WIL,
V'HA SHANA HABA' AH

Home

After Mr. Pig married Selma Pig
he said, "My dears, we must
have a cozy house to live in."
"We have my house in town,
and your house in the country,"
said Mrs. Pig.
"They are both
cozy and homelike."

"That's just it," said Mr. Pig.
"I'm not sure which house
feels most like home."

"Why don't we try them both?" asked Mr. Pig's son, Sonny.

"We can stay in town one week, and in the country the next. Then we will know which house feels most like home."

"Very good," said Mr. Pig.

"But I must take my easy chair and reading lamp.

No house can
feel like home
without them."

Mr. Pig piled
his easy chair and reading lamp
into a cart, and they started
off to town.

The cart creaked and hummed
as it rolled along, and
Mr. and Mrs. Pig and Sonny
hummed and sang along with it.
After a while it started to rain,
but no one minded a bit.

When they were almost in town,

Sonny said, "Oh dear,

I've left my goldfish bowl

and bongo drums in the country.

No house can feel like home

without them."

"And I've left my favorite

books," said Mr. Pig.

So they turned around and

went back to the country.

Mr. Pig piled the goldfish

bowl, the bongo drums and the

books on top of the easy chair

and the reading lamp.

"Now," he said, "we're ready

to roll. Where is Mrs. Pig?"

"Here I am," said Mrs. Pig.

She came out of the house

carrying a large bundle.

"This will make you feel

even more at home," she said.

She piled Mr. Pig's tea set, his
curtains, his footstool and his
cuckoo clock on top of the cart.
"How thoughtful of you,
my dear," said Mr. Pig.
And they started off again.

The cart creaked and groaned
as it rolled along.

Rain trickled down their
ears and off their noses.

But the little Pig family sang
so merrily that no one minded.

When they were

almost there,

Mr. Pig said,

"Oh dear,

we must go back to the

country once more!

I've forgotten my slippers.

No house can feel like home

without my slippers."

So they turned

around once

more.

The cart creaked and groaned
and moaned and squeaked as
they splashed through the mud.
Rain trickled under their
collars and down their necks.
But the little Pig family
sang so cheerfully that
no one minded a bit.

Suddenly, the cart broke down.

The books, the curtains, the tea

set, the drums, the goldfish, the

chair, the footstool and the lamp

fell in the mud

right under a tree.

"Cuckoo! Cuckoo! Cuckoo!"

sang the cuckoo clock.

"How nice," said Mr. Pig.

He sat down on his easy chair

and put his feet on the footstool.

"It's three o'clock and

time for tea."

"It *is* cozy and dry," said Sonny.

He hung his jacket on a branch,

and started to bong on his drums.

"This is quite homelike,"

said Mrs. Pig.

She held up the teapot

to catch rain

for tea.

"Did you say homelike?"

asked Mr. Pig.

"Yes, you dear Pig,"

said Mrs. Pig. "It doesn't

matter where we are. As long

as we're together it will

always feel like home!"

So they sat and had tea

right under the tree.

And no one minded the rain a bit.

Always Waiting

One morning Mr. Pig

woke up tired.

First he opened one eye.

Then he opened the other eye.

Then he closed them both

and sighed.

"Oh," said Mr. Pig,

"I am so tired."

"Why are you so tired?"

asked Mrs. Pig.

"Didn't you sleep well?"

"I slept very well,"

said Mr. Pig.

"But I am still tired."

"Maybe you are getting sick,"

said Mrs. Pig.

"That's it," said Mr. Pig.

"I am getting sick.

I am getting sick and tired

of waiting!"

"What are you waiting for?"

asked Mrs. Pig.

"I am always waiting for
something," said Mr. Pig.
"Either I am waiting for
something to begin,
or I am waiting for
something to end."
Mr. Pig sat slowly up in bed.

"Oh, I am tired of waiting," said Mr. Pig.

"Always waiting for something to start, or waiting for something to stop."

"Which one are you waiting for now?" asked Mrs. Pig.

"Both," said Mr. Pig.

"I am waiting to start eating breakfast so I can stop being hungry."

"Breakfast is ready!" called Sonny Pig.

"Oh lovely!" said Mr. Pig.

"No more waiting!"

He got dressed quickly,

and ran down to breakfast.

Sonny Pig brought in
orange juice and eggs,
cereal with honey and raisins,
buttered toast and jam,
pancakes and maple syrup,
and a large pitcher of milk.
"There," said Mrs. Pig, "now
you won't be tired anymore."

Mr. Pig started to eat very fast.

He gulped down

his juice.

He slurped down

his eggs.

He bolted

his cereal.

Then he stopped

and burped.

"Oh dear," he said. "Now

I *am* sick and tired!"

"I know why you are sick,"

said Sonny.

"But why are you tired?"

"Because I have to wait for

breakfast to end,"

said Mr. Pig,

"so I can begin waiting

for lunch."

"Stop being such a pig,"
said Mrs. Pig. "If you ate
your breakfast more slowly,
you wouldn't have to wait
so long for lunch."
"You are right," said Mr. Pig.

He put jam on his toast, and
ate it slowly. It tasted good.
He buttered his pancakes, and
poured maple syrup on them.
They tasted good.

They tasted so good

that he loved every bite!

"Oh," said Mr. Pig, "I don't

want breakfast ever to end!"

Then Mr. Pig stopped waiting.

He stopped waiting

for things to begin.

He stopped waiting

for things to end.

And he never started again.

Soup for Supper

"Mr. Pig," said Mrs. Pig, "I am making soup for supper, but I need carrots and peas. Will you go to the market and get some?"

"I wish the market was in our back yard," said Mr. Pig. "Then I could take a mud bath while I got the carrots and peas."

"We could grow our own food
in the back yard if we
planted seeds," said Mrs. Pig.

"Good," said Mr. Pig.

"I will get some seeds at
the market and plant them."
Mr. Pig got lots of vegetable
seeds at the market.

"This will certainly make
delicious soup," he said.

He went home and dug a

big hole in the back yard.

Then he threw all the

seeds in the hole.

He threw in string bean seeds,

carrot seeds, squash seeds,

and little baby pea seeds.

"What are you doing?" asked his son, Sonny Pig.

"I am planting our own food," said Mr. Pig.

"That's not the way to plant a proper garden," said Sonny. "You have to plant the seeds all in a row."

"But I'm not planting a garden,"
said Mr. Pig.

"I am planting vegetable soup."
Mr. Pig poured some water
into the hole and stirred
it around.

Then he dipped his finger

into the water and tasted it.

"Doesn't taste right," he said.

"That's because it is not soup,"

said Sonny. "If you want the

seeds to become vegetable soup

you need sunshine and rain."

"I never heard of putting

sunshine and rain in

vegetable soup," said Mr. Pig.

"But if that's what it needs,

I shall certainly put some in."

He tasted the water again.

"Could use a little salt

and pepper, too," he said.

He went into the kitchen

to get the salt and pepper.

Mrs. Pig was cooking soup

in a large pot.

"Where are the peas and

carrots?" she asked.

"Don't worry, my dear,"
said Mr. Pig. "I have put
pea seeds and carrot seeds
into a hole in the yard.
Now we need sunshine and rain
and a little salt and pepper,
and we can grow our own
vegetable soup."

"But it won't be ready for
supper," said Mrs. Pig.
"Seeds need a lot of growing
time before you can have
vegetable soup."
"Not ready for supper!"
cried Mr. Pig. "But I
am getting hungry!"

"That's all right,"
said Mrs. Pig.
"The soup I
am making is
almost ready."
"Will it be good
even without
carrots and peas?"
asked Mr. Pig.

"Of course," said Mrs. Pig.
"And someday, if you have
planted the seeds properly,
we will have vegetables from
your garden for our soup."
"Properly?" asked Mr. Pig.

"Do you mean all in a row?"

Just then Sonny came in.

"All of the water has drained

out of the hole in the yard,"

he said, "and the seeds are

stuck in the mud at the bottom!"

"Oh good!" said Mr. Pig.
He ran outside and
jumped in the mud.
The seeds stuck
all over him.

Then Mr. Pig rolled
up and down
the yard in rows.

"What are you doing?"

called Mrs. Pig.

"I am taking a mud bath,

planting the seeds properly,

and we still can have

soup for supper!" said Mr. Pig.

Father Pig

"Mr. Pig," said his new wife

Selma Pig, "how would

you like to be a father?"

"A father?" asked Mr. Pig.

"But I am a father.

I have a son, Sonny Pig."

"Yes," said Mrs. Pig. "And soon

you will be a father again."

"Oh good," said Mr. Pig.
"Then Sonny will have
someone to play with."

"Yes," said Mrs. Pig.

"Soon Sonny will have

a half sister.

Or maybe he will have

a half brother."

"A half brother?"

cried Mr. Pig.

"What will the other half be?"

"Don't be a silly pig,"

said Mrs. Pig,

and she went upstairs

to have her baby.

Mr. Pig went into

the garden to wait.

Along came his friend, Crow.

"What's the matter,

Mr. Pig?" said Crow.

"You look worried."

"I am," said Mr. Pig.

"My son Sonny is going

to have a half brother,

and I don't know what

the other half will be."

"Maybe it will be a pumpkin,

you silly pig," said Crow.

And he flew off cawing.

"A pumpkin!" said Mr. Pig.

"How peculiar.

I don't think Sonny

will like that."

Mr. Pig's
friend Rabbit
came down the
garden path.

"What's the matter, Mr. Pig?"
asked Rabbit.
"You look worried."

"I am," said Mr. Pig.
"My son Sonny is going
to have a half brother,
and the other half might
be a pumpkin."

"You don't say,"

said Rabbit.

"Half pig, half pumpkin.

Sonny will not take

very kindly to that."

And he hopped

away laughing.

Just then,
Sonny came
running out
of the house.
"Guess what?"
he yelled.

"I've got

two new

half brothers!"

"Two of them!"

cried Mr. Pig.

"Oh dear me!"

He ran into the

house to look.

There was Mrs. Pig

with two pink little piglets.

"What do you think of your
new twin sons?" she asked.
Mr. Pig breathed a sigh
of relief.

"How clever of you, my dear,"
he said, "to have worked it
all out so nicely."
"Whatever do you mean?"
asked Mrs. Pig.

"Well everyone knows
two halves make a whole,"
said Mr. Pig.

"So now that Sonny has *two*

half brothers,

they are *whole* pigs

of course!"